Dear Pig Fans,

Pigs On The Ball: Fun With Math and Sports is the fifth title in the Pigs Will Be Pigs™ math series. It's all about GEOMETRY! When I was in elementary school, that word frightened me, as did just about everything that had to do with math. I never realized that math was all around us in our daily lives. That's why I wrote the Pigs Will Be Pigs books, which (by the way) are all based on true family adventures. My family loves miniature golf, and every time we play I notice all the different shapes of the greens. One day I had a great idea: This would be a fun way to learn geometry. So follow these easy steps:

1) Read **Pigs On The Ball** just for fun!

2) Go back and read the story again. Look for words like **straight line, edge, angle, equal sides, parallel, semicircle,** etc. Then look at the pictures. Every time a word about geometry is used, you'll see it in the illustrations.

3) Have fun with geometry and food. Which of your favorite foods can you match with geometric shapes? For example, a whole pizza is a circle, and a pizza slice is a triangle. What other shapes can you find?

4) Answer the math questions at the end of the book. You can do this by yourself, with your parents, or with your teacher.

Remember the Pig Family Motto:

MATH + READING = FUN

Love,
Amy Axelrod

P.S. For Parents and Teachers Only
The Pigs Will Be Pigs books have been designed around the National Council of Teachers of Mathematics's Thirteen Standards. Use them as picture book read-alouds initially, and then as vehicles to introduce, reinforce, and review the concepts and skills particular to each title.

Pigs  on the Ball

Fun with Math and Sports

story by **Amy Axelrod**

pictures by **Sharon McGinley-Nally**

Simon & Schuster Books for Young Readers

Mr. Pig had ants in his pants.

"Are we there yet?" he asked impatiently. "I can't wait to see my surprise."

"No peeking," instructed the piglets.

Mrs. Pig pulled into the parking lot. "We're here!" she announced.

"Happy Birthday, Dad," wished the piglets.

"Wow," exclaimed Mr. Pig. "I've been waiting for this place to open."

"Since golf's your game," said Mrs. Pig, "we decided to have your party here."

"Great idea," said Mr. Pig, "except you forgot one thing."

"What's that?" asked the piglets.

"My lucky shirt," he said. "It's at home. I can't play without it."

"No problem," said Mrs. Pig, as she and the piglets each handed him a gift-wrapped box.

"Oh," said Mr. Pig, "a new shirt."

"It's a new *lucky* shirt," said the piglets. "And lucky socks and knickers, too."

"Well," said Mr. Pig, "in that case . . .

COUNT

The Pigs selected their clubs and favorite colored golf balls.

"What a difficult course," commented Mrs. Pig. "Look at all those shapes."

"Piece of cake," said Mr. Pig. "Just remember to putt from one point to the next and pay close attention to the curves and lines of the greens."

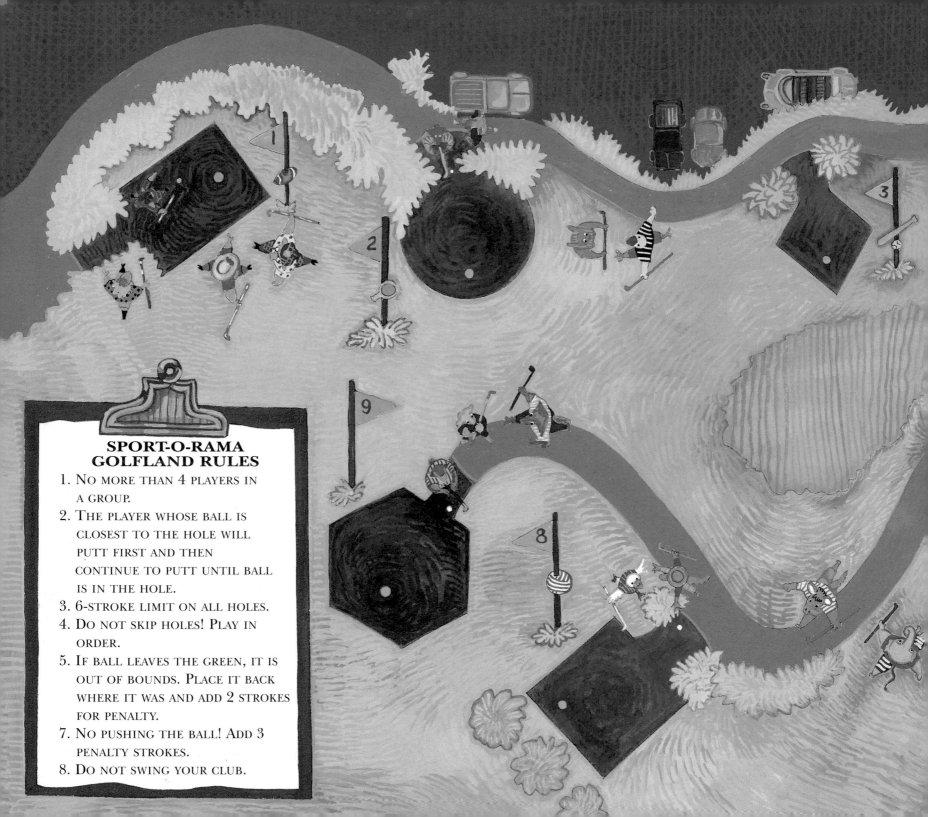

**SPORT-O-RAMA
GOLFLAND RULES**

1. NO MORE THAN 4 PLAYERS IN
   A GROUP.
2. THE PLAYER WHOSE BALL IS
   CLOSEST TO THE HOLE WILL
   PUTT FIRST AND THEN
   CONTINUE TO PUTT UNTIL BALL
   IS IN THE HOLE.
3. 6-STROKE LIMIT ON ALL HOLES.
4. DO NOT SKIP HOLES! PLAY IN
   ORDER.
5. IF BALL LEAVES THE GREEN, IT IS
   OUT OF BOUNDS. PLACE IT BACK
   WHERE IT WAS AND ADD 2 STROKES
   FOR PENALTY.
7. NO PUSHING THE BALL! ADD 3
   PENALTY STROKES.
8. DO NOT SWING YOUR CLUB.

"Nice going, Mom. A hole in one!" cheered the piglets, when Mrs. Pig tapped her ball in a straight line right into the cup.

"I guess that's what you call beginner's luck," joked Mrs. Pig.

"Now watch me," said Mr. Pig, as he stepped up to putt. "Winning that free pizza will be a breeze."

But his ball rolled under the goal post, hit the opposite edge of the green, and rolled right back out.

"Well, that was almost a hole in one," said Mr. Pig after he sunk the ball on his second try.

"Almost doesn't count, dear," said Mrs. Pig.

The Pigs proceeded to hole number two. The piglets and Mrs. Pig had no trouble landing their balls on the green on their first go-around.

"I seem to be losing my touch," Mr. Pig complained the second time his ball overshot the green and wound up in the bushes.

The Pigs moved on to hole number three. "You'd better give me the maximum score," Mr. Pig told Mrs. Pig, after his angle shot propelled the ball out into the parking lot. "It would be rude of me to hold up the line."

The Pigs followed the numbered flags.

"Dad, this one is so easy," said the piglets. "Just gently putt to the center of any one of the equal sides, and the ball will land in the cup."

Mr. Pig tried six times.

"Dear," said Mrs. Pig, "I don't recall the children saying anything about aiming for the corner sand traps."

REFRESHMENTS

The piglets were hungry, so the Pigs took a quick snack break at the end of hole number four.

"Sweetie, do you think my new golf shirt is unlucky?" Mr. Pig whispered to Mrs. Pig. "I'm simply not playing up to par today."

Mrs. Pig shook her head no. "Don't be silly," she said. "You're trying too hard to win that contest. Just relax and have fun. It's your birthday."

At hole number five, Mr. Pig pushed his ball along one entire side of the green.

"That'll cost you three penalty strokes, dear," said Mrs. Pig.

The piglets putted parallel to each other at the sixth hole. Their balls landed in the cups on the first shot. "Two more holes in one!" they yelled.

Mrs. Pig carefully putted and scored the same. But Mr. Pig kept whacking his ball a little too hard.

"Gee, Dad," said the piglets, "too bad we're not scoring basketball."

The Pigs played on.

"Now, do as I did," Mrs. Pig instructed Mr. Pig, after her ball gently rolled around the semicircle of the green and plopped in the cup.

Mr. Pig stretched to loosen up before he putted . . .

. . . but it didn't help. His ball got lost in the water. "Maybe we should have bought you a bathing suit instead," said the piglets.

The other golfers watched Mrs. Pig skillfully putt at hole number eight. The ball traveled at right angles directly into the cup.

"What a pro!" The crowd applauded.

The Pigs were finally at the end of the course.

"I'm calling it a day," said Mr. Pig. "Why even bother here? I'll just toss my ball into the return hole."

"Dad, you can't quit," said the piglets. "We only need one more hole in one."

"The children are right," said Mrs. Pig, as she gave him a big kiss on the cheek. "That's for good luck."

Mr. Pig tightly gripped his club and lined up his shot.

"Look, Dad!" said the piglets. "Here comes your birthday cake!"

"Make a wish," said Mrs. Pig.

"I wish I were eating my cake right now," Mr. Pig thought to himself, as he pulled back to putt.

"C'mon, Dad," encouraged the piglets,
"you can do it. Remember, golf is your . . ."

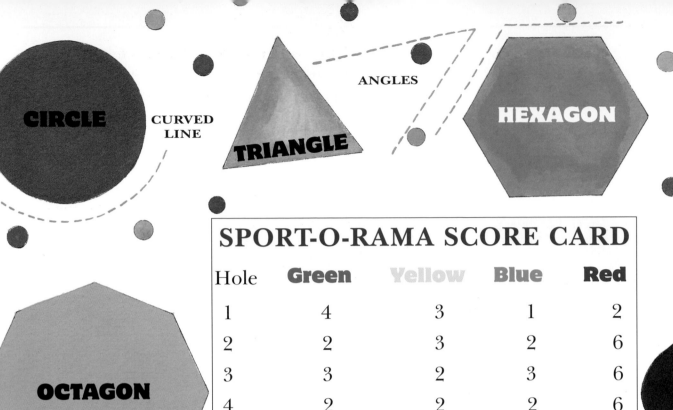

CIRCLE

CURVED LINE

ANGLES

TRIANGLE

HEXAGON

RIGHT ANGLE

SQUARE

OCTAGON

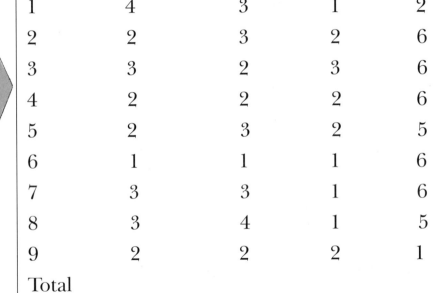

SPORT-O-RAMA SCORE CARD

Hole	Green	Yellow	Blue	Red
1	4	3	1	2
2	2	3	2	6
3	3	2	3	6
4	2	2	2	6
5	2	3	2	5
6	1	1	1	6
7	3	3	1	6
8	3	4	1	5
9	2	2	2	1
Total				

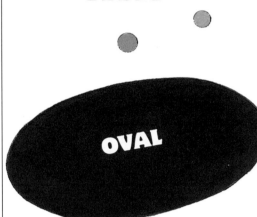

OVAL

RECTANGLE

RHOMBUS

STRAIGHT LINE

SEMICIRCLE

PARALLEL LINES

Tally the miniature golf scores for the Pig family. Who came in 1st? 2nd? 3rd? 4th? Remember that in golf the lowest score wins.

Can you think of everyday objects that have the same geometric shapes as the golf greens?

Which shapes of the greens have all equal sides? 2 equal sides? 3 or more equal sides? no equal sides?

Bonus question: How many times did Mr. Pig actually putt at holes #2 and #5?

For my Bram,
who always remembers
to wear his lucky golf shirt

—A. A.

For Christopher Michael McGinley,
born August 12, 1997.
Welcome to the world.

—S. M-N.

First Aladdin Paperbacks edition August 2000
Text copyright © 1998 by Amy Axelrod
Illustrations copyright © 1998 by Sharon McGinley-Nally

ALADDIN PAPERBACKS
An imprint of Simon & Schuster Children's Publishing Division
1230 Avenue of the Americas
New York, NY 10020

Designed by Anahid Hamparian

The text for this book was set in 17-point Baskerville.

The illustrations were done in inks, watercolors, and acrylics.

Manufactured in China

10 9

The Library of Congress has cataloged the hardcover edition as follows:

Axelrold, Amy.
Pigs on the ball : fun with math and sports ; written by Amy Axelrod ; illustrated by Sharon McGinley-Nally.
p.   cm.
Summary: The Pig family visits a miniature golf course and learns about shapes, angles, and geometry.
ISBN 978-0-689-81565-2 (hc.)
[1. Shapes–Fiction. 2. Geometry–Fiction. 3. Miniature golf–Fiction. 4. Golf–Fiction.
5. Pigs–Fiction.]
I. McGinley-Nally, Sharon, ill. II. Title
PZ7A96155Phe 1998   [E]–dc21   97-39776
ISBN:978-0-689-83537-7 (Aladdin pbk.)
1013 SCP